FLAMINGO is BRAVE

A book about feeling SCARED

Written by Sue Graves

Illustrated by Trevor Dunton

W
FRANKLIN WATTS
LONDON • SYDNEY

Flamingo was scared of lots of things.
He was scared of **spiders**.

He was scared of **the dark**.

4

He was scared of **loud noises**, too.

At school, he was scared of playing football. He was scared he might kick the football **the wrong way**.

He was scared of **reading out in class**
even though he was a really good reader!

At playtime, Flamingo was scared of playing hide-and-seek. He worried he **might get lost**.

When Flamingo got scared, he hid his head under his wing. He shivered and shook and his knees knocked together in fright. Flamingo didn't like being scared. He wanted to **be brave**.

On Friday, Monkey had some **exciting news**. It was his birthday the next day and everyone was invited for a sleepover in his garden.

Everyone was excited. Everyone except Flamingo.
He was scared. What if a **spider** got in the tent?
What if it got **too dark**? What if they played
hide-and-seek and he **got lost**?
Flamingo was sad.

Flamingo went to find Grandpa. Grandpa was
busy in the garden. He told Grandpa his worries.
He said he wished he could **be brave**.
Grandpa said when he felt scared he pulled back
his shoulders and lifted up his chin. He said he
took a **deep breath**, too.

Flamingo pulled back his shoulders and lifted up his chin. He took a deep breath. Flamingo felt **a bit better**.

Grandpa said everyone got scared sometimes. He said when he was a little bird he was **scared of swimming**. Flamingo was surprised. He **liked swimming** very much. It was fun!

14

Grandpa said he thought the water **looked scary**. He said his friends helped him. He soon **loved swimming**.

Flamingo said he could ask his friends to help him.

Grandpa said that was a great idea.

15

Flamingo went to see his friends.

He told them his worries.

He said he wanted to be brave.

His friends said they would **help him**.

16

The next day, it was Monkey's party.
First of all, they played hide-and-seek.
Flamingo felt scared. He remembered what
Grandpa had said. Flamingo pulled back his
shoulders, lifted up his chin and took a deep
breath. He **felt better**.

Everyone joined in the game. Everyone had fun. And Flamingo **didn't get lost** at all.

Soon it was time for bed. Suddenly a spider ran across Flamingo's bed.

20

But Monkey showed Flamingo how to catch
the spider in a glass.
Flamingo **wasn't scared at all**.

It got darker and darker. Flamingo worried that it would get **too dark**. But Tiger lent him his torch and the dark **wasn't scary at all**.

Everyone said Flamingo was being **very brave**.

Just then, everyone heard a strange noise.
Everyone thought it was a monster **and hid**!
But Flamingo pulled back his shoulders,
lifted his chin and took a deep breath.
He peeped outside the tent.

24

It wasn't a monster at all. It was Monkey's big toy tractor and that wasn't scary at all. Everyone laughed and said Flamingo was **very brave!**

Flamingo was proud. He liked being brave.
It was much better than being scared!

A note about sharing this book

The **Behaviour Matters** series has been developed to provide a starting point for further discussion on children's behaviour both in relation to themselves and others. The series is set in the jungle with animal characters reflecting typical behaviour traits often seen in young children.

Flamingo is Brave
This story looks at some of the typical things that may scare children and investigates strategies for overcoming fears.

How to use the book
The book is designed for adults to share with either an individual child, or a group of children, and as a starting point for discussion.

The book also provides visual support and repeated words and phrases to build reading confidence.

Before reading the story
Choose a time to read when you and the children are relaxed and have time to share the story.

Spend time looking at the illustrations and talk about what the book might be about before reading it together.

Encourage children to employ a phonics first approach to tackling new words by sounding the words out.

28

After reading, talk about the book with the children:

- Talk about the story with the children. Encourage them to retell the events in chronological order.

- Talk about the things that scare the children. Point out that many of their fears are experienced by others and are especially common amongst children. Invite the children to share their fears with the group.

- Talk about how fears can be allayed. Many children like to have a night light on if they are scared of the dark. Others like to have a favourite toy to take to bed. Encourage the children to share their ideas for coping with fears. Take the opportunity to share your own childhood fears with the children and explain how you overcame them.

- Point out the strategies mentioned in the story. Grandpa got his friends to help and encourage him. He also shows Flamingo how to pull back his shoulders, lift up his chin and take a deep breath. Invite the children to stand up and try that procedure for themselves. How does it make them feel?

- As a class, invite the children to help you write a list of the things that worry them. Ask the children to suggest ways of overcoming each fear. Leave the list on display for future reference.

For Isabelle, William A, William G, George, Max, Emily,
Leo, Caspar, Felix, Tabitha, Phoebe and Harry – S.G.

Franklin Watts
First published in 2020 by
The Watts Publishing Group

Text © Franklin Watts 2020
Illustrations © Trevor Dunton 2020

The right of Trevor Dunton to be identified as the illustrator
of this Work has been asserted in accordance with the
Copyright, Designs and Patents Act, 1988.

Editor: Jackie Hamley
Designer: Cathryn Gilbert

A CIP catalogue record for this book is available
from the British Library.

ISBN 978 1 4451 7089 3 (hardback)
ISBN 978 1 4451 7090 9 (paperback)

Printed in China

Franklin Watts is a division of
Hachette Children's Books,
an Hachette UK company.
www.hachette.co.uk

MIX
Paper from
responsible sources
FSC® C104740
FSC
www.fsc.org